8725

This document of identity is issued with the approval of His Majesty's Government in the United Kingdom to young persons to be admitted to the United Kingdom for educational purposes under the care of the Inter-Aid Committee for children.

THIS DOCUMENT REQUIRES NO VISA.

PERSONAL PARTICULARS.

Name OPPENHEIM DORRITH MARIANNE

Sex FEMALE   Date of Birth 8/12/1931

Place KASSEL

Full Names and Address of Parents

OPPENHEIM Hans & Gertrud

Kaiserstr. 59

KASSEL

This side is reserved for official use only:—

LEAVE TO LAND GRANTED AT HARWICH
THIS DAY ON CONDITION THAT THE HOLDER
DOES NOT ENTER ANY EMPLOYMENT
PAID OR UNPAID WHILE IN THE UNITED
KINGDOM

IMMIGRATION OFFICER
(8)
26 JUL 1939
HARWICH

To Andrew, who gave me so much support,
and for our children and grandchildren —D. M. S.

Thanks to Becky and Debbie —G. F.

I was seven and a half on July 26, when my visa was stamped.
By the start of World War II, on September 3, 1939, almost
ten thousand children had fled to Britain through organized
Kindertransports out of Nazi Europe. We had done nothing
wrong, but most of us were Jewish and we weren't safe in our
homes.

In Scotland, I learned English, new customs, and a new way
of life. After the war, I longed for news about my parents. I had
to wait for a long time. Sadly, many of the children didn't see
their parents again. Fifty years later, Kindertransport groups
meet in many different countries to educate others about what
happened, and to continue helping family members find one
another, even now.

—D. M. S.

Requests for permission to make copies of any part of the work should be mailed to:
Permissions Department, Harcourt Brace & Company,
6277 Sea Harbor Drive, Orlando, Florida 32887-6777.

First published 1996 by ABC, All Books for Children, a division of The All Children's Co. Ltd., London
First U.S. edition 1997

Library of Congress Cataloging-in-Publication Data
Sim, Dorrith M.
In my pocket/written by Dorrith M. Sim; illustrated by Gerald Fitzgerald.
p. cm.
Summary: Fear and uncertainty afflict everyone on the boat on the morning in
July 1939 when Jewish children sail from Holland to the safety of
a new life in Scotland.
ISBN 0-15-201357-1
1. World War, 1939–1945—Jews—Rescue—Juvenile fiction.
[1. World War, 1939–1945—Jews—Rescue—Fiction. 2. Jews—Europe—Fiction.
3. Voyages and travels—Fiction.] I. Fitzgerald, Gerald, ill. II. Title.
PZ7.S58855In 1997
[E]—dc20 95-52469

A C E F D B

Printed in Singapore

In my pocket

Dorrith M. Sim

ILLUSTRATED BY Gerald Fitzgerald

HARCOURT BRACE & COMPANY
San Diego   New York   London

Hardly anyone on the boat ate breakfast that morning.
It was 1939.
It was July.
And I was on a boat.
A boat full of children escaping from danger.

Back at the Hamburg railway station,
a train had been waiting.
Waiting to take us to Holland,
to the boat.
Mutti and Vati told me the boat
would take us to a new life.
The parents cried.
We cried, too.

I dropped my toy dog.
It lay on the tracks.
A man rescued my dog.
He called, "Catch!" as he threw it to me.
Right after I caught it, the train began to move.
I stopped crying and clutched my dog as I waved good-bye.

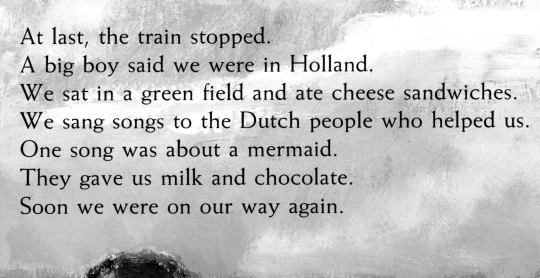

At last, the train stopped.
A big boy said we were in Holland.
We sat in a green field and ate cheese sandwiches.
We sang songs to the Dutch people who helped us.
One song was about a mermaid.
They gave us milk and chocolate.
Soon we were on our way again.

On the boat, it was strange sleeping without my parents.
Only brothers and sisters knew each other.
In the night, some children got lost.
They left their cabins to look for the bathrooms,
and they could not remember their way back.

Then it was time to leave the boat.
We wore name tags around our necks.
There was a wooden bridge.
Looking through the slats at the sea made me dizzy.
I didn't want to move but everyone behind pushed me.
I shut my eyes and held the rail.
I shuffled forward with my eyes closed.
At last, my feet touched the ground.
That's when I started to cry.

A train stood ready.
Someone said it was a British train,
taking us to London.
Many people were at the station.
Some children had friends or
family to meet them.
Others looked around for help.
There were men with cameras,
and people holding photographs.
Those people had promised to
take children into their homes.
The children were to be part of
their families until they could be
with their own parents again.

A man and a woman studied a photograph.
The wife touched her husband's arm.
"Look," she said. "The girl with the red
ribbon in her hair and the big toy dog."
That's how they found me.

A man with them spoke German.
He said, "Willkommen schön Kind."
The couple spoke English.
All I could say was,
"I have a handkerchief in my pocket."
That's how I began to teach myself.
Whenever I learned a new word,
I put it in the same sentence.
"I have a dog in my pocket."
"I have a house in my pocket."
"I have a teacher in my pocket."

The man and woman came from Scotland.
Everything there was different.
In Germany, I sat on a little seat on my father's bike.
In Edinburgh, where they lived, there was a car.
And I had a real dog.

In Germany, I couldn't play in
our street with other children
because I was Jewish.
Now I played with my
new Scottish friends.
Soon I was calling the woman
and man Mummy and Daddy.
I saved Mutti and Vati
for my real parents.

I got a letter from Mutti and Vati.
"We miss you so much.
Remember to be good.
And don't forget to write to us.
This morning we picked mushrooms
and thought about you. We hope to
be with you very soon."
I hoped so, too.
I kept Mutti and Vati's letter.
I read it every day.
I kept it with me,
safe in my pocket,
until there was no more war.